The Legend of the Amulet's Dragon

O. R. Yen

ISBN: 9798638809409

Dedicated to Athena, my little pants ninja.

In memory of my great grandma Ruth.

CONTENTS

ACKNOWLEDGMENTS

A big thank you to my mom and dad, my sister Athena, Grammy, and my cats and dog and lizard, for helping me, encouraging me, inspiring me, and also for being my family. An even bigger thanks to my mom and Grammy for typing this up and to my dad for helping me with the cover.

CHAPTER ONE

The lemurs shrieked overhead as Lexnon, or "Lex" for short, ran through the Madagascan rain forest. Lex was twelve years old, and was part of a tribe of ninjas who lived on Madagascar known as the Vi'kawi. The Vi'kawi were enemies of a tribe of warriors called the Di'vori, who want to destroy the Vi'kawi because some people are just jerks in that way.

So, Lex had decided to search for the legendary Amulet of Altuka, a mystical relic said to make the wielder the master of a giant dragon! Unfortunately, as Lex searched the ancient temples and ruins, he had come across some Di'vori warriors.

And that was what Lex was running from right now. He panted as he ran through the lush jungle vegetation. He was out of breath and gasping for air, as if he were a deflated balloon, desperately trying to re-inflate himself.

Suddenly, the five Di'vori warriors who had been chasing him burst out of the undergrowth. Lex ran into a clearing trying to get away from the evil warriors, but they surrounded the clearing.

Lex groaned: "Oh no!" He took his two swords out from their cases on his back and twirled them over his head, glaring at his opponents. He then let out a loud, coyote-like battle cry, lunging at two of the warriors.

Lex kicked one in the stomach and slapped another in the face with the flat side of his sword and they fell down. Then Lex tripped a warrior and that warrior knocked into another warrior and both warriors fell down. Then the last warrior snuck up behind Lex and kicked him from behind. Lex turned onto his back and watched helplessly as the Di'vori warrior was about to slice him in half.

Suddenly, a ring-tailed lemur jumped out of a tree, onto the last Di'vori warrior's head, and began screeching and tearing the warrior's hair out.

"What the...?" said the warrior. "What is wrong with you?!" he yelled.

"Thanks Zeke!" said Lex. Zeke the lemur had been friends with Lex ever since Lex once saved Zeke from a forest fire.

The warrior stumbled and Zeke leaped off the warrior's head, pushing the warrior into a thorn bush.

"Good job, Zeke!" said Lex. "Now let's get out of here!"

"That was a close one," said Lex after a few minutes of running through the jungle. "We really should go home n....hey, is that a temple?"

CHAPTER TWO

It really was a temple! The archway above the door said:

This is the ancient Temple of Toukaka,
home to the legendary Amulet of Altuka

"You know what?" said Lex. "I have a feeling the amulet is in here."

Zeke nodded. So they both went in.

~~~~~~~~~

Deep underground, under the Temple of Toukaka, a legendary creature awoke from its thousand-year slumber. It shook the layers of dirt and rock off its scaly body. The dragon had awoken!

~~~~~~~~~

Meanwhile, back above ground, Lex and Zeke had entered the temple. It had pillars made of brown stone that were covered in ivy. Vines draped down from the ceiling like chandeliers. The ancient building was pyramid shaped. Torches lined the walls and at the top of the temple there was a large hole that let a beam of light through. That beam of light shined onto a platform and on that platform there was...the Amulet of Altuka!

This is the ancient
temple of
home to the legendary
Amulet of

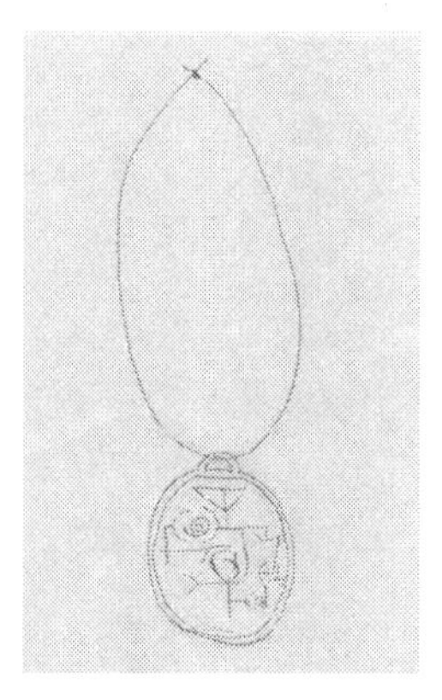

It was just lying there, in the hands of a statue of a sitting, cross-legged, giant panda. It would have been quite easy for Lex to pick up the Amulet, had it not been for the acid moat surrounding it. Luckily, there was a stone bridge; however, there was no railing, so if Lex slipped, he would probably fall into the acid.

He carefully crossed the bridge and made it on to the platform. Now his hand was only a yard from the legendary relic...a foot...an inch...a centimeter...a...KA-BOOM!!

Suddenly, the Dragon burst out from underneath the temple!

It was as if someone had activated a bomb below the ancient structure. Giant stone blocks, dirt, and acid went flying everywhere.

So did the Amulet of Altuka.

Lex tried to grab it as it hurled through the air while he dodged a blob of acid and the amulet landed in a pile of rubble. But Lex didn't have time to search for it. First, he had to get out of the temple. He tried to run for the door, but a massive stone block smashed in front of it.

"This is not good." said Lex. "Not good at all."

Luckily, Lex happened to look up and spot the hole at the roof. He grabbed Zeke and started to climb a vine wrapped around a pillar. Unfortunately, the Dragon saw him, so it blasted the pillar with fire.

The ivy and vine were set aflame. Lex jumped off of the vine he was on, and onto another vine that was dangling from the ceiling. Then Lex swung back and forth, back and forth, back and forth, back and forth...until he swung forward really far, let go, shot through the hole as if he had been fired out of a cannon, and landed safely on the roof of the temple.

"That was definitely a close one!" said Lex.

Zeke screeched in agreement. But little did they know that another danger was lurking nearby in the trees.

CHAPTER THREE

Meanwhile, far away from the Temple of Toukaka, in the Di'vori village, the Di'vori were getting ready for war.

They strapped swords onto their back, stuffed daggers into their belts and boots, and sharpened their axes. The chief of the Di'vori, a man named Chief Chudon, watched his warriors prepare for the attack on the Vi'kawi through the window in the tower he was in.

He was tall and muscular, covered in scars, and all his clothes were made of black leather. He also had an eye patch over where his eye had been a long time ago.

He stared down at his axe. One blade was smooth, shiny, beautiful diamond. The other was rough, black obsidian.

He watched his warriors work from the tower. He slowly and menacingly chuckled. "Those annoying Vi'kawi shall soon be no more than a distant memory," he said in a voice as rough as sandstone.

Then he sunk his axe deep into the table he was sitting at.

~~~~~~~~~

Meanwhile, back on top of the temple of Toukaka, Lex was trying to form a new plan to get the Amulet. "OK," he finally said, "here's the plan. First we're gonna…"

"Shriek, shriek!" shrieked Zeke, interrupting Lex in the middle of his sentence.

"Zeke!" yelled Lex. "Stop interrupting me!" But Zeke kept screeching and jumping everywhere and pointing behind Lex.

"OK, fine," said Lex. "I'll look at whatever you want me to see."

He turned around and saw the warrior that had fallen into the thorn bush. The warrior was covered in scratches from the spikes. He was missing some hair, thanks to Zeke, and the hair he did have had lots of twigs and leaves stuck in it. He scowled at Lex and Zeke.

"We meet again." he said.

Lex jumped onto the branch the warrior was on and
~~~~~~~~~

smashed into him. The warrior plummeted down to the ground, hitting every branch on the way down.

Suddenly, the four other warriors Lex had fought in the clearing jumped from above onto the branch Lex was on. The weight of the warriors, Lex, and Zeke (who had also jumped onto the branch) was too much for the branch to bear. It snapped and Lex and the warriors plummeted to the ground. Zeke had jumped to the nearest branch at the last minute.

Lex grabbed onto a warrior that was grabbing onto the dagger that he had sunk into the tree that they had fallen from. Lex grabbed the handle of the dagger as well and kicked the warrior off. The warrior plummeted to the ground, just like the others had.

Lex used the dagger to pull himself onto the branch Zeke was on, like a rock climber. Then, when he had successfully pulled himself onto the branch, he yanked the dagger out of the tree and tucked it safely in his boot, just in case. Then they hopped back onto the roof of the temple.

"Okay," said Lex, "back to my plan to get the amulet. First we have to…" He was interrupted again by even MORE warriors that jumped out from the trees. One of them pointed a sword at Lex's throat.

"Aw, man," moaned Lex. "I thought I had defeated all of you guys."

The Di'vori pointing a sword at Lex's throat slowly lowered his weapon.

"Greetings," he said. "I am Commander Crossfire. Chief Chudon wanted us to find the five Di'vori warriors that were on patrol and mysteriously disappeared. We managed to track them here and watched you defeat them. Now you must pay!"

He leaped toward Lex, prepared to sink his sword into him. Lex stumbled backwards and fell through the hole in the top of the temple. He screamed as he fell down to his certain doom.

Zeke and the warriors peered down and saw that Lex had grabbed the end of a vine at the last second, dangling just meters over the stone brick floor.

Unfortunately, his screaming caught the attention of the dragon. It had been on the other side of the temple when it heard the screaming. Its head snapped toward the sound. It blasted a stream of fire at Lex. Lex scampered up the vine like a monkey, barely dodging the thick blast of fire. The blast hit the roof of the temple and half the ceiling caved in.

Lex, Zeke, Commander Crossfire, the warriors, and a bunch of giant stone blocks plummeted down to the ground.

Luckily, Lex grabbed Zeke and the dragon's tail right as the dragon slithered into the hole in the floor it had made when it burst out from under the temple.

CHAPTER FOUR

Under the temple it was dark. And damp. And kind of smelly.

Lex and Zeke watched the dragon. First it seemed to be sniffing around for something. Then it let out a loud eardrum-shattering roar. It waited for a minute before being responded to by another, more distant roar.

The dragon watched the entrance of a dark cavern. Slowly, an even larger dragon stepped out of the darkness of the cavern. The first dragon was red and black. The second dragon was purple and green.

At first, Lex just stared at the dragons softly roaring and growling at each other when something sparkly caught his eye.

It was the Amulet! The dragon must have brought it down here so I couldn't get it, thought Lex.

"Stay here," Lex told Zeke. Lex slowly crept out from behind the stalagmite they had been hiding behind. He slowly tiptoed around the side of the cave. He was just about to snatch the amulet when the larger dragon spotted him. It let out a blast of fire. Lex quickly grabbed the amulet, scrambled away from the flames, and put the amulet around his neck.

The smaller dragon's eyes started to glow white. It was possessed.

The larger dragon was about to open fire on Lex when the smaller dragon blasted the ceiling. Boulders fell from the top of the cave like hail. They sealed the bigger dragon out from the rest of the cave.

After the big dragon was taken care of, Lex grabbed Zeke and got on the dragon's back. The dragon flapped its wings and took off. It flew out of the temple, which was quite easy because half of the roof had caved in.

As he flew away from the temple of Toukaka, Lex felt an indescribable joy. It was true joy. Pure joy.

"Woo-hoo!" yelled Lex as the dragon flew through a cloud. He patted the dragon's head.

"I think I'll name you Burn," he said.

As they flew high above the jungle towards the Vi'kawi Village, Lex smelled something burning.

"Hey, I smell smoke," commented Lex. Zeke nodded and pinched his nose. As they drew closer to the Vi'kawi Village, the smell got stronger, too. Soon they saw smoke billowing out of a large patch of trees.

"Oh, no," said Lex. "We're not in time to stop the attack because the attack has already started!"

CHAPTER FIVE

The Vi'kawi village, unlike the Di'vori village, was a treehouse village. The huts were built into the trees and connected by large wooden pathways. Usually they were used for getting around, but currently they were being used for battling. Oh, and half the village was on fire.

Later this would be known as the battle of the flaming trees, the concluding battle of the Vi'kawi-Di'vori civil war.

Hang on! I can't tell you about the Vi'kawi village without telling you about the Di'vori village!

OK, the Di'vori village was in a giant clearing. It was surrounded by a wall made of vertical logs, a moat, catapults, and watchtowers. There was only one entrance, a portcullis with at least four guards patrolling it at all times.

Nobody knows why the Di'vori are so protective of their village. They just are.

Good, now that I've told you about that, I can get back to what I was doing. Now, where was I? Oh yeah, I remember now.

So anyway, the Di'vori and Vi'kawi were battling each other. Lieutenant Lightranger and his squad of elite units had even been sent. And they were only used in emergencies.

Lieutenant Lightranger was currently locked in combat with a Di'vori commander. He finally managed to throw the commander off the pathway. Suddenly, he heard the beating of enormous wings. He looked up and saw a colossal red and black dragon with glowing white eyes! Upon further inspection he realized there was a person and a ring-tailed lemur on the dragon's immense tree trunk neck.

Up on Burn's neck Lex shouted, "Quickly! Blast the bad guys, Burn!"

Burn nodded and blasted at a group of warriors. The warriors ran away from the flames licking at their heels, hoping for a taste of boot. One particularly unlucky warrior had his butt set on fire. He scooted around on his butt desperately trying to extinguish the fire. When Burn flew down so Lex could see the warrior with his butt on fire, Chief Chudon leaped out of the trees, drawing his diamond and obsidian axe. Lex drew his swords.

The fight was on!

CHAPTER SIX

Burn flew higher into the sky as Lex and Chief Chudon dueled. Chief Chudon hurled his axe at Lex. Lex managed to deflect it with his swords. The axe cartwheeled through the air.

It was about to plunge into Chief Chudon's face when Chief Chudon calmly reached out and grabbed the handle of the axe, the diamond blade just half a centimeter from his face.

Chief Chudon swiped his axe at Lex. Lex barely managed to jump over the sharp blade.

After a long battle, sunset started to arrive. Suddenly, an extremely deafening roar as loud as thunder shook the earth. And it wasn't from Burn.

All of a sudden, the other, slightly larger dragon Lex had fought beneath the temple of Toukaka burst out from the trees. It was about to blast Lex, Chief Chudon, and Zeke into smithereens. But then it looked at the possessed Burn and held its fire. It clearly didn't want to accidentally hurt Burn.

It started circling Burn.

"Go away, you hideous beast!" yelled Chief Chudon.

The dragon snarled and spewed a blazing hot fireball. It hit Burn in the back. Burn roared in agony and hurled out of control towards a jagged mountain. As they crash-landed on the cliff of one of the mountains, the amulet of Altuka slipped off of Lex's neck and shattered on the cliff.

CHAPTER SEVEN

"NOOOO!!!!" screamed Lex!!!

Burn's eyes stopped glowing. Burn was no longer possessed.

Chief Chudon, who was standing at the edge let out his slow and menacing chuckle. "Looks like you're not so tough without a possessed fire breathing war-machine."

Lex glared at him, but then a light bulb went off in his brain. He remembered something he had put in his boot for safekeeping earlier. He slowly drew the dagger out of his boot.

Before Chief Chudon knew what was going on, Lex threw the dagger at him. It spun through the air, like Chief Chudon's axe. The handle of the dagger hit Chief Chudon right on the nose.

Chief Chudon stumbled backwards and nearly fell off the cliff. He stuck out his arms to steady himself, like a tightrope walker. He slipped and fell off the cliff to his doom below.

CHAPTER EIGHT

Lex turned towards Zeke and the dragons. The larger dragon nuzzled Lex with its snout. Lex patted the dragon's head.

"I'll name you Blaze," said Lex.

Lex walked past Blaze towards Burn and Zeke. And they weren't alone. There seemed to be a weird purple and red boulder. Hold on! That wasn't a boulder! It was an egg!

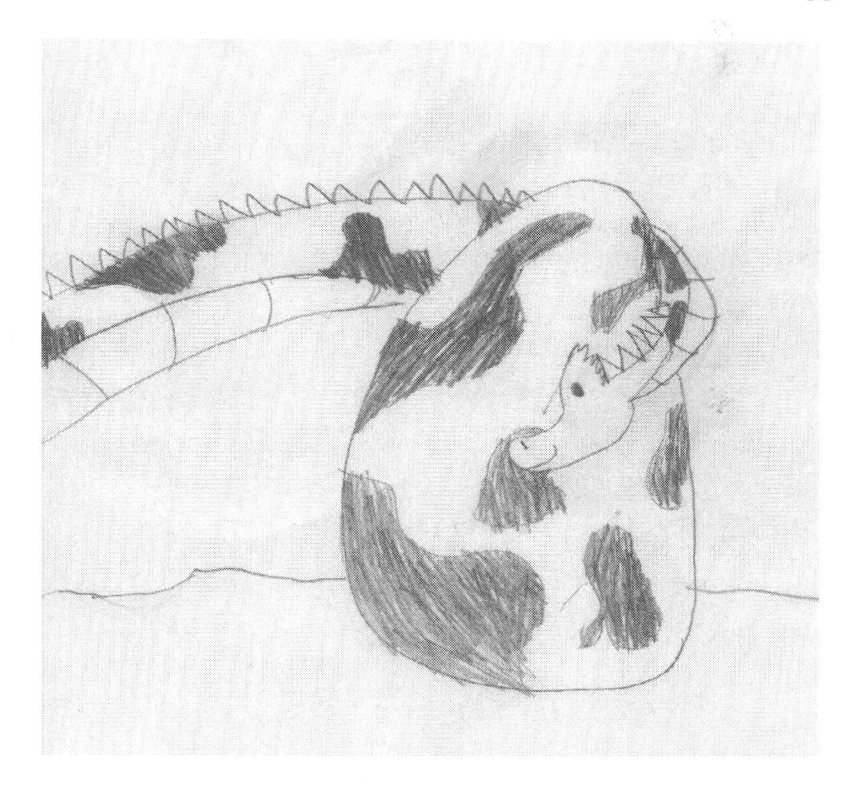

Burn had laid an egg!?! What!?!

"Hang on a minute," said Lex. "Does that mean…". He looked at Burn, then at Blaze, then at Burn again. "Ew," said Lex.

Crack! Burn, Blaze, Lex and Zeke stared at the egg.

Crack! The egg cracked again. And again. And again! All of a sudden, the egg exploded! Tiny bits of eggshell rained down on them. When the dust settled, there was an adorable purple and red baby dragon.

"Aww," said Lex. "Hey, little guy." The baby dragon burped out a tiny little flame. "I'll name you Scorch," said Lex. Zeke nodded and screeched in agreement.

Scorch waddled over to Burn and Blaze and licked them with his forked tongue. The three dragons flapped their wings and flew towards the setting sun. As Lex and Zeke watched the dragons flying into the sunset, towards the temple of Toukaka, Lex bent down and picked up something. It was Chief Chudon's obsidian and diamond axe. As he stared at the sunset and the dragons, he sensed that Chief Chudon was (probably) gone for good.

CHAPTER NINE

Now, that sounds a lot like an ending. And it would have been, had it not been for one unfortunate turn of events. The "probably" in the parenthesis was there for a reason, you know.

Okay, here's what happened: when Chief Chudon fell off the cliff, he had grabbed onto the edge of it. And Lex had somehow not seen the fingertips hanging over the edge of the cliff. Chief Chudon suddenly hoisted his chest and stomach onto the cliff and grabbed Lex's ankle. Surprised, Lex looked down and saw his archenemy glaring back up at him.

"If I'm going down," growled Chief Chudon, "then you're coming with me!"

All of a sudden, the cliff collapsed for no reason at all, and the three of them plummeted down to the ground far, far, below. Chief Chudon grabbed his axe and was about to stab Lex with it and Lex had nothing to defend himself with! His swords had fallen out of their scabbards when Lex had smashed into the cliff.

Just as the blade was about to pierce his skin and sink into his flesh, three streams of fire shot out from behind Lex and blasted Chief Chudon to smithereens.

At the sight of their leader exploding, all the Di'vori warriors dropped their weapons and put their hands in the air in surrender.

Lex looked over his shoulder and saw Burn, Blaze and Scorch flying towards him. Burn caught Lex on her back and Lex saw Zeke on Blaze's back and Scorch flying beside them.

Then Burn, Blaze and Scorch took them down to the Vi'kawi village. And they all lived happily ever after.

The End
(almost)

EPILOGUE

The village threw a giant feast that lasted two weeks. Because of their victory, they made that day, March 14, a holiday. And now, five years later, if you find an ancient temple, you just might find a family of dragons.

ABOUT THE AUTHOR

O.R. Yen is in fourth grade. Yeah, you heard me. He's only in fourth grade! This is his first book he has ever written (so far!).

He lives in Northern California with his one mom, one dad, one little sister, one dog, two cats, a lot of fish, and a lizard.

Made in the USA
San Bernardino, CA
04 May 2020

70673849R00018